DOWN AND OUT IN PARIS, WITH CAT

This title is number two in the Frayed Edge Press Street Smart Series, published irregularly starting in 2019.

Other titles in the series include:

Full Fare by Jean-Bernard Pouy

The Accidental Anarchist by A.R. Melnik

Stealing MacGuffin by Matthew Kastel

Pele's Domain by Albert Tucher

DOWN AND OUT IN PARIS, WITH CAT

R. A. Bolo

Frayed Edge Press
Philadelphia, PA

Publisher's Cataloging-in-Publication Data

Names: Bolo, R.A.
Title: Down and out in Paris, with cat / R.A. Bolo.
Description: Philadelphia, PA : Frayed Edge Press, 2019. | Series: Street smart series ; 2 | Summary: An American ex-patriot leads a life that many would envy: living and working in Paris. But all is not well for him in the beautiful "city of lights"—his French girlfriend has left him, he's fallen off the wagon after decades of sobriety, and a homeless cat is now tugging at his heartstrings.
Identifiers: LCCN 2019946626 | ISBN 9781642510133 (pbk.) | ISBN 9781642510140 (ebook)
Subjects: LCSH: Americans--France--Fiction. | Anarchists--Fiction. | Cats--Fiction. | Paris (France)--Fiction. | Poor—France--Fiction. | BISAC: FICTION / Animals. | FICTION / City Life. | FICTION / Political.
Classification: LCC PS3602.O56 D69 2019 | DDC 813 B6--dc23
LC record available at https://lccn.loc.gov/2019946626

For Georgie

Yeah, I know—for a lot of people, it would seem like I was living the dream life in the beautiful "city of lights" of Paris. I'm sure it looked that way from the outside: cushy, well-paying job as an English-language researcher; sexy young French girlfriend; cheap rent for a decent apartment owned by my girlfriend's aunt in the nearby suburb of Noisy-Le-Sec; easy commute of just two stops on the RER Magenta line from *Gare du Nord*; and access to all the sights and sounds and food and activities that Paris has to offer. And the food—did I mention the food? Not just the butter and cream-infused concoctions that the French are known for, but the variety of meats I could get on a regular basis from the local butcher: entrails, goat, horse. Shocking to friends and family back home in the States, but I have to admit that I really like horse. To me, there's no difference between eating a horse and eating a cow, and the French know it. I appreciate that streak of no-nonsense in them. If it were possible to make billions by factory-farming horses, or if it weren't only the rich who could keep and love a pet horse, nobody would give a second thought to *les boucheries chevaline*.

So, yeah, it was a regular "life of Riley" in Paris for me, except that it wasn't. I'd left Boston and moved to be with Marie-France in Paris after my Boston girlfriend Julie threw me out of the house. Julie's a smart, hard-working academic, but way too possessive and controlling, and way too intolerant of a minor indiscretion like Marie-France. Julie always had to be talking about and negotiating "the relationship" and it all just got too heavy. As for me, I'm an anarchist and more of a free love advocate, which I really think is better for everyone involved. Julie argued that it wasn't really "free love" or polyamory if everyone involved didn't agree to it, and I could never get her to see my point of view. Then she found out about Marie-France and kicked me out.

So, I found myself on the other side of the Atlantic, living with Marie-France, and to be honest, Julie was starting to look good to me again. I mean, Marie-France definitely had her points. She was young and energetic in bed, and she was an artist and musician with a lot of creative ideas. But she was perpetually encased in a cloud of smoke and it seemed like something on fire was always in her hand, whether it was a *Gitanes*, a clove cigarette, or a joint. It may have been the language difference, as neither of us was completely fluent in the other's native tongue, but I was also irritated by the shallowness of her intellect and her constant retreat into the creative process. I'd come home from work and the apartment would be a disaster area with dirty laundry piled up and the kitchen covered in paint, but nothing to eat and no food in the refrigerator.

"What have you been doing all day?" I'd bark at her, waving the smoke out of my eyes. "I've been working my ass off and I'm ready to eat!"

"I've been *painting*, darling," she'd reply languidly, as if there was all the time in the world and no need to worry about eating. At that point, I'd storm out of the apartment and go to the café down the block and order something to eat. Then I'd walk the streets of Noisy-Le-Sec enjoying the sounds of music slipping out the doors of some of the clubs. I'd look into the eyes of some of the African immigrants who I'd pass on the street, wondering if they could possibly feel more alienated and alone in France than I did. Then when it was late enough that I was sure that Marie-France had gone to bed, I'd finally go home, sleep, wake up the next day, and do it all over again.

After living in this state of non-conjugal non-bliss for several months, it turned out that Marie-France was the one with the lowest tolerance for our constant bickering. I arrived home to the apartment one evening to find her gone, along with a good portion of her clothes and art supplies. There was a note on the paint-spattered kitchen table that read, "Darling, I just can't take it any longer, off to stay with mes amis en Rouen, talk later, ciao, MF." A sent of clove cigarette lingered in the air. I left the apartment and headed to the café once again.

After Marie-France had fled, I was afraid I'd have to move out of the apartment; we'd been paying extremely cheap rent for it because it belonged to her aunt, Marie-Anne. But Marie-Anne completely understood what a flighty, pain-in-the-ass Marie-France could be and offered to lower the rent even more since it was only me living there. I kept her happy in return by making my handyman skills available on weekends for help around the apartment building: re-writing a light fixture, replacing a rotted window sill, clearing a blocked drain.

But things seemed to start a steep downward slide after this. Julie refused to take my late-night, long-distance calls and I heard from Boston friends that she was dating someone else. The few phone calls I had with Marie-France started out friendly enough, but ended with tears and angrily slammed phone receivers. Even though it was the proverbial "springtime in Paris," the "*Temps des cerises*" or "time of the cherry blossoms" that intoxicate with feelings of love and perhaps revolution, the weather seemed unnaturally cool and the Paris sky was perpetually overcast, which perfectly matched my mood.

Then one evening, I was eating at the usual café and there happened to be a new waiter on duty serving me. I was a "regular" there by now and all of the waiters knew me—and knew that I didn't drink. But this new guy didn't know that, and he was pushing me.

"Mais, pourquoi pas, monseiur?" he asked, aggressively pushing the wine list in my face. I was either going to punch the guy or order some damn wine. I ended up doing the latter, breaking over twelve years of sobriety. After that, the steep downward slide turned into a plunge off the cliff.

My job of course started to suffer. I was late almost every day, I called out sick a lot or just didn't bother to show up, and when I did come in, I was hungover and surly, and not in a mood to get much work done. My boss Marie-Claude went from being an occasional grouch to being a full-time bitch. She was laying on the passive-aggressive schtick big time, with every interaction being, "Could you *please* do this" or "Thank you *so very much* for that." I couldn't stand being there but it was a paycheck, even when they were docking my pay for missed hours. It was obvious Marie-Claude wanted to fire me, but she needed my native-English-speaker skills until the research project we were working on was over. I knew I had job security, at least for a while.

Then my health began to suffer as well. My paycheck was getting smaller and a good portion of it was going for booze. I couldn't afford to eat out, so I had to go shopping and try to cook for myself. I started to wait in line with the other poor immigrants for charity handouts of food once a week, just so I'd have some food on hand and more money for booze. I couldn't afford to pay to heat the apartment, so it was cold all of the time. I was getting sick on a regular basis and had a perpetual cough that I just couldn't shake.

At night, I'd often walk out in the streets, too angry and agitated to stay at home. Sometimes I'd try to chat with a prostitute or another drunk that I'd encounter on my walks, but usually the language barrier and my own impairment prevented any meaningful communication. My normal pattern was to stumble back to my apartment after midnight and try to get some sleep, but on more than one morning, I was awakened by an angry shopkeeper or resident who found me passed out in their alley or doorway. Once I was even picked up by the police, but was released with a stern warning after playing the part of a poor, ignorant foreigner.

My dream life in Paris was turning into a real nightmare. Every day on the train platforms on my commute to and from work, it seemed like at least one of the schedule-boards would post a thirty-minute delay on one of the train lines, due to an *"accident du personne."* This meant that someone had jumped in front of a train. I wasn't quite ready to buy that ticket, but I started to understand the feeling, to get a whiff of why it was such a common event in France.

Then one evening when I was walking home from the train station, a bright spot entered my life. I took a slightly different route home and, on the street that was behind the street that I lived on, I noticed a house with a *clos*, or enclosed garden, where someone had put food out for the street cats. There was a black-and-white mother cat there with three half-grown kittens, all having their supper on top of the stone wall. Seeing them made me so totally, inexplicably happy that I almost cried right there on the street.

I stopped on the sidewalk next to the wall and watched them as their little pink tongues lapped up the food left on an old, chipped plate. They reminded me of cats that my family had taken care of in our yard when I was growing up. I also had bittersweet thoughts of cats of my own that I'd had as an adult—some lost long ago to disease or old age, some left behind in Boston when I had moved. Watching these cats made me feel so good that I went home and cooked a delicious stew of chunks of horse meat and vegetables. I stayed inside all night, and only drank a little.

Passing by the house that fed the cats then became part of my regular routine and I'd often see the mother cat and her kittens there eating. There were some other street cats that would show up there as well: a crusty old grey tom who the mother cat would give a wide berth to, a grey tabby of indeterminate sex, and a couple of youngish calicos that looked like they could be sisters. The people feeding the cats appeared to be a young family consisting of father and mother and two or three young children. I'd sometimes here the kids yelling and playing in the yard, or the parents calling out to them from the house. It seemed like such an idyllic situation—a young, healthy, happy family caring for cats who needed their help.

Visiting the cats at the wall became the high point of my day, and made my bleak existence a little less bleak. I started sticking a can of sardines in my pocket when I left for work in the morning, and then opening it up to share with the cats on the wall on my way home. They were gradually getting used to me, and would react when they saw me coming. Some of the older ones were even open to letting me pet them. Eventually I started hoisting myself up to sit on top of the wall, petting and playing with the cats, and grabbing the kittens to hold them and try to socialize them so they'd be less feral. Everything else in my life was still pretty much

*Visiting the cats at the wall became the high point of my day,
and made my bleak existence a little less bleak.*

sucking, but being with these cats gave me one glimmer of hope and purpose.

Then one day, that came crashing down as well. I stopped by the wall on my way home as usual, but when I got there I was shocked by a new development. A hand-drawn sign on a plain white piece of paper, that looked like it had probably been made by one of the children, was taped to the wall. It read: "Rester loin de notre mur!"—which means, "Stay off of our wall!" An unhappy or angry face was drawn at the bottom. The message was clear: my presence was not welcome, and the joy I received from interacting with the cats was now at an end. This simple sign felt like a punch in my gut, and I avoided walking down that street from then on.

The weeks rolled by, and I was adrift in a black sea of depression and hopelessness. My drinking increased, my attendance at work decreased, and my health (which had actually been improving) was now taking another nose-dive. I was coughing so much and so hard that it would sometimes keep me awake at night. I was never sure if I had a fever or not, but I always felt kind of low-grade terrible. I was surly and argumentative and would snap at anyone I interacted with. Life was not good.

One day when I'd actually managed to make it into work, Marie-Claude stopped by my cubicle with a young, well-dressed man. His dark hair was perfectly styled, he wore trendy fashionable glasses, and he exuded that kind of energy and exuberance found only in the young. I hated him on sight.

"This is Jean-Philippe," Marie-Claude told me, and I grudgingly shook the young man's hand. "He may be doing some work for us in the future and I'm showing him around the office. Would you *please* take a few minutes to speak with him and explain what it is that you do here? Thank you *so much*!" And off she went without even waiting for a reply from me.

Jean-Philippe pulled another chair into the cubicle and sat there beside me, asking some questions about the work I did and dotting the conversation with some information about himself. It turned out that he had studied in the United States for a few years and his English was actually pretty good. I answered his questions in the most basic ways possible, not going into much detail unless he specifically asked. Then it finally dawned on me why he was here: he was someone Marie-Claude was considering as my replacement.

Once that lightbulb turned on, I turned off. I got shorter in my responses and ruder in my demeanor until he finally took the hint, thanked me politely, and left to track down Marie-Claude. Later in the day, when I was sure that Marie-Claude was within earshot, I loudly said to Marie-Thérèse in the cubicle next to mine: "Hey, what's up with that guy Jean-Philippe? He seemed like a nice enough fellow, but his English is *absolutely terrible*!" We never saw Jean-Philippe after that. I had won this round, but I still had enough brain cells left to know that I'd only won a battle and not the war. My days on the job were numbered and Marie-Claude would eventually take me down.

A feeling of desperation started to set in. I was a hopeless drunk in a foreign country where I didn't speak the language, had difficulty in navigating my day-to-day activities, and had no hope of finding another job once this one ended. I'd never get a good recommendation from Marie-Claude and there wasn't a lot else I could do. Sometimes at night, I'd drunkenly walk along the canal, staring into the dark waters and wondering if it wouldn't be better if I just threw myself in and ended it all.

Just as my despair was becoming more palpable, and the thought of the dark canal waters embracing me was becoming more comforting, I was once again saved by an angel on four furry feet. The kitchen window in my apartment looked into the small backyard of our building. I happened to glance out of it one day, and I noticed a young, scrawny, black-and-white cat sitting on the wall at the back of the yard. I'm not really sure that he could even see into the window, but it seemed at the time that he was looking straight at me. I felt an immediate need to spring into action. I grabbed some leftover food from the refrigerator, and took it out on a small plate to the backyard.

The cat eyed me warily from his perch on the wall. He didn't come for the food when I set it down, but he didn't run away, either. He watched me closely and waited until I left. Then I could see from my window that he'd come for the grub, gobbling it down hungrily. That evening I bought a bunch of cans of cheap cat food and began a new routine of feeding the little guy every day.

I gradually went about trying to gain his trust. First, I stopped going all the way back into the building after I set the food down; I'd just go to the door and wait. He could still see me there, but his desire to eat made him brave enough to come down from the wall and enter the yard for the food. Then I started to just sit on a bench in the yard, after leaving the food about halfway between the bench and the wall. The cat was still hungry enough, and starting to see me as less of a threat, that this arrangement was acceptable to him as well. I'd talk to him in a soothing voice while he ate, trying to help him get used to me. He didn't seem to mind this, but he still wasn't drawn into contact with me; he'd leave the yard as soon as he was finished eating.

After about a week of this, I sat on the bench and put the dish of food next to me, then waited. If he wanted to eat, it would cost him a head scratch this time. Sure enough, the beast crept up to his dish and ate while I petted him and scratched his furry head. Our real friendship began at that time. He was now open to interacting with me, and would run to greet when I entered the yard in the evening with his food. Now he would hang out with me even after he finished eating, lounging on the bench next to me and waiting for head scratches and belly rubs. Seeing him close up, I noticed the distinctive teardrop-shaped white blaze on his chest, and knew that he was one of the kittens from the litter I'd played with at the house at the far end of the block. He was almost fully grown now, probably about ten months old.

As I continued to feed my new black-and-white buddy on a regular basis, he filled out and put on weight. He was no longer a scrawny, skinny little cat, but a strong, healthy-looking feline with some meat on his bones. Pretty soon he'd be ready to own the neighborhood, or at least our small section of it. But there's a funny thing about cats sometimes. We think we're helping them out, that we're rescuing them, but it actually turns out that at the same time, they're also rescuing us. I now had something to distract me from my sorrows; I had someone to come home to and something to look forward to every night.

Things were looking up all around. Ever since the Jean-Philippe incident at work, I'd made more of an effort to make it into the office every day and to get at least some work done while I was there. I had another mouth to feed and that was an incentive to put the hours in and get as full a paycheck as possible. Marie-Claude seemed to appreciate my new-found work ethic and eased up on the bitchiness somewhat. I knew that my position there was still in jeopardy, but I now felt more hopeful about the future. I was drinking less, spending more of my money on food and less on booze, and I no longer entertained dark thoughts at the side of the canal.

I was generally in a better mood all around, and Julie even started taking my calls again. She was still seeing the guy she'd started dating after I left, and I think that gave her enough confidence to re-open contact, keeping me clearly in the "friend zone." It was great to chat with her and she loved to hear stories about my new cat friend. Being a real "cat person" herself, she always had news of her own cats, as well as of some of our mutual friends back in Boston. Talking to her helped give my life another sense of normalcy, and provided a tie to the happier times back home. I never told her that I'd fallen off the wagon, but I was sometimes drunk when I was talking to her and I imagine that she had begun to suspect.

So, I'd managed to establish a new, more sustainable pattern in my life—but it wasn't long before that, too, got thrown off the rails. One evening in mid-November, I brought the cat food out to the yard as usual but there was no cat there. I was disappointed, but I didn't think too much about it at the time. I figured my cat buddy was "otherwise engaged" elsewhere, and would show up the next day, hungry as usual. But he didn't show up the next day, or the day after that. Three whole days went by without any trace of him. I tried not to think of it as a rejection but consoled myself somewhat with the thought that, "Well, either he's been adopted by somebody else or he's been squashed by a Peugeot." I continued to hold out hope of seeing him again ("maybe he was accidentally locked in someone's basement!") but in truth a bit of light had gone out of my life once again.

On the Friday afternoon following the cat's disappearance, I had come home early and was startled to hear a long, horrible moan through my rear window. I looked out and there was my *chat du rue*, stumbling across the yard, falling on his side after every two or three agonized steps. This was accompanied by the most pathetic, heart-rendering, drawn-out yowling that I had ever heard: "Mmmmmrrrraaaaaaooooowwwww!!!" I rushed down to the yard, snatched up the poor, suffering beast and brought him inside. He kept trying to stand but continued to topple over on the kitchen floor. There was no obvious evidence of injury or blood, and I could find no broken bones as I felt along his legs and body. I was in a real panic and not sure what I could do to help him. I threw an old sweater into a box and put him in it, hoping that he might settle down. Unfortunately, the cat's distress and his awful yowling continued.

I knew absolutely nothing about veterinary care in France, so I figured that I needed to find someone who did. I tried to call Marie-France, but she didn't answer. I was then desperate enough to do something I really didn't want to do, which was to call my work colleague Marie-Thérèse and ask for her advice as a favor. Marie-Thérèse spoke English well enough and she'd always been friendly to me, if a little distant. I managed to reach her, and between what she knew and the advice that her boyfriend chimed in with, I got some useful information for next steps to take.

It sounded like the vet school would be my best bet; I called and they said that they would be willing to see the cat free of charge if I got him there before 5 PM. Unfortunately, the school was on the opposite side of Paris from me, and I'd have to change trains at least a couple of times after getting to the city. It was not likely I'd make it there on time. Plan B was to take him to the local vet in Noisy-le-Sec, which luckily happened to be open that evening.

I carried the groaning cat in the cardboard box as a cold, steady rain started to fall on the lamplit streets. A young veterinarian, a man who I could see was not the boss, and a young woman who seemed to be in training, received us. I explained the situation in my clumsy French as they began to examine my little friend. The verdict was that he'd probably gotten into a poison trap for rats or mice that someone had left in a shed or basement. Ingesting this kind of poison was unfortunately commonly fatal for stray cats. They said that they could hydrate him with an intravenous line and if he survived the night and didn't show signs of too much organ damage, they'd castrate him the next day and give him back to me. If he was too badly damaged, they would just euthanize him.

The quote that they gave me for their services was more money than I even had. I think that they could tell that by the shocked look on my face. In return, I gave them my sob story about being a poor immigrant and asked how much they would charge for just the minimum life-saving treatment. They conferred together quietly and seemed to take pity on me, but said that ninety euros was the best they could do, dead or alive. That was about three quarters of everything I had in the bank, but I agreed.

The following afternoon I returned to the vet's office and, to my delight, there was my brave critter, all cleaned up and standing on his own four feet. I thanked the vets profusely, paid them, and brought my boy home. Unfortunately, "NO PETS" was one of Marie-Anne's iron-clad rules for the apartment. She had endless horror stories about how woodwork had been damaged or carpets "absolutely destroyed" by thoughtless pet owners and their filthy, vicious animals. When we moved into the apartment, Marie-France had to turn over custody of her beloved pet snake to a former boyfriend. Once, after we'd been there a few months, I'd asked Marie-Anne about having some small, caged animals like hamsters or guinea pigs in the apartment. She had looked at me in horror, imperiously declaring "NO RODENTS!"

So, I knew I was wantonly breaking one of the cardinal rules for having access to the cushy deal for this apartment. But it was almost like I didn't really have a choice; it was really a life-or-death situation that called for protecting an endangered friend. I named him Georgie that night, after the son of George Brown, a long-dead anarchist of Philadelphia who I'd researched and written about during the preceding year. George Junior was born in 1892 and had a fairly idyllic childhood, but he had returned from the Great War shell-shocked and alcoholic, leading a dreary life thereafter. It was a little surprising to think that the cat had remained nameless this long, but now he was here in the apartment with me and the name seemed to fit.

The cat's journey back to health continued through his first night indoors. Georgie paced the floors growling, avoiding me, and only nibbling at his favorite food that I put down for him. I went to bed, hoping that he would feel more settled by morning. In the middle of the night, I was awakened by a thump as he jumped up on the bed, and I was gratified to feel him curling up by my feet. It was cold in the apartment due to my non-payment of the heating bill, and even if he was scared and disoriented, he knew where to find warmth. We both drifted back off to sleep. Later in the wee hours of the morning, I was awakened by him again as he started scratching at the comforter on my bed. It wasn't the loving kind of kneading that cats do, but rather the kind of digging they do when they are ready to do their business. Realizing he was getting ready to have a crap, I jumped out of bed and grabbed him. As I carried him to the kitchen where I had left a makeshift litter box, he was dropping small, hard turds along the way. The vets had warned me that the poison he'd eaten may have made him constipated; this was his painful moment of "clearing the pipes."

In the morning, he did seem more settled and he undoubtedly felt better physically after having gotten rid of the bad crap that had plugged him up. Being the fastidious genius that most cats are, he immediately recognized the value of the litterbox and never had another "accident." I now officially had a pet in an apartment where pets were strictly prohibited; Georgie was now an indoor cat and my new best friend.

We fell into a new routine where I would arrive home from work, lie down on the couch, and softly call his name. He would immediately appear and jump up onto my chest, and I'd pet his purring body and stare into his round, dark eyes. Georgie had long, black fur with two white paws in the front, a narrow white mask on his face, and the distinctive white teardrop blaze on his chest; I was in awe of his beauty. After cuddling on the couch and relaxing from my day, we'd both have dinner together. I was still drinking too much at night, but at least I was no longer drinking alone. I had Georgie for company, and he was never judgmental.

Despite the joy that my new friend brought to my life, I was still struggling and in a constant state of anxiety. I was trying to make it into work every day, as much as I could, and trying to draw as much pay as possible. But I'd finally gotten an official letter of dismissal from the "big boss,"

We fell into a new routine where I would arrive home from work, lie down on the couch, and softly call his name. He would immediately appear and jump up onto my chest, and I'd pet his purring body...

Marie-Claude's superior, thanking me profusely for my contributions to the project, while at the same time stating in no uncertain terms that my services would no longer be required once the project ended. I estimated that I had another six to ten weeks on the job, and made the conscious decision to slow my pace at work to help ensure that number was as close to ten as possible. I also had to take steps to economize again, saving as much money each week as I could and only buying the cheapest food for both myself and Georgie. I was once again standing in line for the charity food handouts at a *Resto du Couer*—"Restaurant of the Heart," coming home with a sack of rice, some wilted vegetables, an odd assortment of canned goods, and some frozen meats. It wasn't the best grub in the world, but it definitely helped.

When I had courage enough to face facts, I knew that this couldn't go on forever. No matter how much I economized, no matter how much free food I stood in line for, no matter how often Marie-Anne "forgot" about the rent in thanks for my small repairs around the building, it just wouldn't, it just couldn't last. My job would eventually end and my money would eventually run out. I saw no hope of finding steady work elsewhere. I had few friends and fewer opportunities on the horizon. I felt completely, utterly stuck. If it hadn't been for Georgie, I'm sure that the idea of jumping onto the train tracks or throwing myself into the canal would have started to look good again.

Then one night, a door cracked open for me. I was talking to Julie on the phone and I know I'd probably been going on at length about all of my problems and how hopeless I felt. I felt stuck and didn't see any way out of my troubles. Julie finally interrupted me, saying, "I have an idea. Why don't you come home?"

"Haven't you been listening?" I'd retorted irritably. "I have sixty euros in the bank. That would probably buy me a second-class train ticket to London from here. If by 'home,' you mean 'Boston,' it's going to be a long swim."

"No one's expecting you to swim!" she snapped back. "I've been talking to Jacob and Alexandria and some of your other friends here. We're willing to spring for a one-way plane ticket back."

"You…you are?" The offer was entirely unexpected and threw me off guard.

"Yes, we are," Julie went on. "We've been talking about your situation and everyone agrees that it would be better if you were back in the States."

"Well, thank you. Let me think about it. It's a generous offer and it certainly has its appeal." We agreed to talk again in a few days, after I'd had more time to think it over.

In the intervening days, the offer of plane ticket back to Boston got even more appealing. My situation in Paris was seeming more and more like a dead end. Back in Boston, I'd have more resources: more friends and more work opportunities. It was looking like my salvation, my way out, had arrived. There was just one problem: what to do with Georgie.

When I next talked to Julie, I told her that I'd gratefully take up the offer of the plane ticket back to Boston. "But I'm wondering about Georgie," I said. "Can he come, too?"

"I've looked into it," Julie responded. "Honestly, it's just not doable. The cost to take him on the plane would be almost as much as a second ticket. You'd have to have a regulation-sized carrier to bring him into the cabin. And he'd also need to have a completed health form from a veterinarian, and even with that, he'd have to stay in quarantine for three months."

"Really?" I asked, trying to take it all in. The thought of another visit to the vet, and paying for it, seemed daunting on the face of it, not to mention having to buy a special carrier.

"Yes," said Julie. "And just think about it from his perspective: how happy would he be on a long international flight? And how happy would he be, sitting in a cage somewhere for three months? He's a French cat; he needs to stay in France. You need to see if you can find a home for him there, or a shelter that will take him."

Julie was always the practical, logical one and I usually heeded her advice on most things. But I really couldn't stand the idea of leaving Georgie behind. I made a mental note to find out how much it would cost to get the medical form from a vet, and to come up with a good plan for paying everyone back if they'd spring for the cost of Georgie's flight. I tried not to think about the quarantine for the time being.

I made some non-committal noises to her in regard to the fate of the cat, and we went on to discuss other aspects of my return to Boston. Julie was now living with her boyfriend, so I wouldn't be able to stay with her. She told me that our mutual friend Damien had a spare room at his place and was willing to put me up for at least a few weeks on my return to Boston. Things were slowly starting to come together for my return to the States.

The next day, I blew off going in to work. Since my time was officially nearing an end there and I had a new plan in place for my next steps, my motivation to do any work at my job had taken a steep nosedive. Instead, I ventured back to the local vet's office to see what I could find out about the needed medical form for Georgie's travel. As luck would have it, the young veterinarian who'd provided Georgie's life-saving treatment was there and available to speak with me. I thanked him again for his help with my poor cat and assured him that he was doing well. As best as I could explain in my poor French, I communicated to him that I planned to return to the U.S. and needed a health form for the cat to travel. In turn, he explained back in a mixture of French and English that he wasn't familiar with this, but that he would look into it and give me a call when he had more information.

After that, I went home and thought about what I'd need to do in order to leave. I'd been in France for over a year and I'd accumulated various possessions in addition to what I'd brought with me. Now I needed to think about how much I could pack into suitcases and what I needed to get rid of. Georgie sat on my bed, watching with intense interest as I went through my clothes.

"What do you think, Georgie?" I'd ask, holding up a sweater. "Pack it or sack it?"

Georgie wasn't particularly opinionated, but that didn't stop my banter with him. "What do you think about moving to the United States?" I asked. "You'll have to learn English, but there's some nice girl cats in Boston that I'm sure will be charmed by your French accent."

I was making progress on creating "keep" and "discard" piles of clothing when my phone rang. It was the vet calling with information about the required animal travel form, and the news wasn't good. It turned out that Georgie would need a complete physical work-up, including blood work and various tests for illness, and would need to get several vaccinations as well. The best price the vet could offer was a hundred euros, more money than I had to my name. I thanked him for the information and told him I'd get back to him.

This news was enough to send me into another dark funk. I spent the rest of the afternoon drinking and trying to figure out a way to make bringing Georgie home with me a reality. But every train of thought I started on ended in a black tunnel with no light at the end. I lay half dozing on the couch with Georgie resting on my chest when the phone rang again. This time it was Julie calling from Boston. She wanted me to give her a departure date as soon as possible so that she could purchase the plane ticket for me.

I normally didn't want to talk to Julie when I'd been drinking because I didn't want her to know that I'd fallen off the wagon. But I was feeling sorry for myself, and sorry for Georgie, and I needed someone to talk to. I told her what the vet had said and she was not particularly sympathetic.

"I already told you that bringing the cat back wasn't going to work!" she said. "I don't know why you're even pursuing this. You need to put your time and energy into getting ready to leave, and that includes finding a home for him."

"I know," I whined. "But poor Georgie! I saved his life! He saved my life! I just can't bear the thought of leaving him! Do you think you could lend me the money to pay for the vet visit for the form?"

That's when Julie lost it. "Listen to me!" she yelled. "I don't think you're fully grasping what's going on here. You can't even take care of yourself! How do you think you'll manage taking care of a cat? Your friends are paying to get you home. We're providing you with a place to stay, and help in getting back on your feet. You need to start cooperating with the people trying to help you, and stop feeling sorry for yourself and coming up with new problems we have to solve for you." At that moment, I knew that she understood the full extent of the trouble I was in.

"You're right," I conceded. "I'm sorry. I do appreciate what you and the others are doing for me. I'm going to work on finding a home for Georgie." I promised to give her a date for my return soon and we hung up. As much as I didn't want to face it, I knew I'd have to be leaving my beautiful boy behind. I buried my face in his luxurious fur and told him, "I'm sorry" over and over again. Then I opened another bottle.

The next day I woke up on the couch with a terrible hangover, but with a gorgeous black-and-white cat still snoozing on my chest. It was almost noon, so there was no room for any thought of going in to work that day. I fixed a pot of coffee, had some "hair of the dog that bit me," and warmed up some leftovers I found in the fridge. After feeding myself and Georgie, I knew I had to accomplish something productive that day.

It seemed to me that there had to be animal shelters somewhere in the vicinity, just like there were back in the States, although I'd never noticed one in any of my travels around the city. But I did some searching online and found what looked like a good bet—a place that was in a nearby suburb and that adopted out dogs and cats. I called the number on the website and in my lousy French, tried to explain my situation to the woman who answered the phone. Between my French and her English, I finally got my message across. But she told me that there was an eighty-euro fee to surrender an animal at their shelter. I could afford that about as much as I could afford the airline ticket for the cat.

It was discouraging to get more bad news, but I also figured there were other shelters in the greater Paris area. Maybe some of them were cheaper or would cut me a deal. I would do more research and make more calls later. Now I needed to get out of the apartment and get some fresh air. I pulled on my coat and walked around the neighborhood for about an hour and then decided to go home by way of

Dominque's house, which was a couple of blocks away from my apartment. She was always happy to see me and I needed cheering up. I also had to let her know that I would be leaving the apartment, and it would be good to get one more task out of the way.

I wasn't disappointed when Marie-Anne answered the door. Her gray hair was pulled back in a neat bun, and she wore a nice dress and jewelry even though she was just sitting around at home—a typical elegant French woman. She broke into a smile when she saw me, saying "Come in! Come in! It's been so long since I've seen you! How come you never visit me?"

"I'm sorry, Marie-Anne," I said, taking off my coat as I entered her small, tidy house. "I've been really busy and I've been having some difficulties. I didn't want to burden you…"

"It's no burden! I'm always happy to see you, no matter how your life is going. Do you want coffee?"

"Yes, I'd love coffee," I responded, following her into the kitchen. I sat at the table while she busied herself getting water started for the coffee. "I'm afraid I have a couple of things I need to tell you, and I'm afraid you're not going to like either of them."

"Oh, no! What is it?" she asked, looking at me with concern. "It's not that wild child Marie-France, is it?"

"No, it's not Marie-France. I haven't spoken to her in months and I'm not even sure how she's doing. I don't think she wants to hear from me."

"That's alright," said Marie-Anne. "You can do better."

I laughed at that, but got more serious when I responded to her. "I have to tell you that I'm going to be leaving the apartment soon. My job is ending and I don't think I'll be able to find more work here. My friends in Boston have offered to buy me a plane ticket home, and I think I'm going to take them up on it."

"Oh, is that all? I thought something was very wrong. Going home is good. That is probably the best thing for you. I'll miss having you here; you've been such a help to me. But don't worry about the apartment—I never have any trouble finding a new tenant. When do you plan to be leaving?"

"I'm not sure; I think in a couple of weeks or so. I need to let my friend in Boston know so she can buy the ticket. But there's another problem as well, and I need to take care of it before I leave."

"What's that?" she asked. She'd brought a loaf of bread to the table and now was pulling a leftover baked ham and some cheese out of her refrigerator. I could always count on Marie-Anne to feed me when I came to her place. Now I wouldn't have to worry about dinner.

"I don't want this to upset you," I told her, "but I have a confession to make. I have a cat in the apartment and I know I'm not supposed to. I'd been feeding him in the yard and one day he got poisoned. It was really terrible; he almost died. I had to take him to the vet and they said he needed to stay inside to recover, and I just…"

"A cat! You know that animals are against the rules!"

"Yes, I know and I'm sorry. I didn't mean to have him inside; it just sort of happened. Now I need to find a home for him before I leave."

"Well, I'm sure you didn't come here thinking that I would take the creature in!"

"Oh, no, of course not. I was just hoping you might have some advice about what I should do. I tried calling a shelter earlier, but I don't have the money for the fee."

"Animal shelters are a scam," replied Marie-Anne. "You don't want to give them money for anything!"

"But what should I do, Marie-Anne?"

"You put up flyers. You say, 'free cat to good home.' Someone will take it."

"Do you think so? That would be great if I could find someone to take him. He's a very nice, very clean cat," I assured her.

We chatted for a while longer, and I ate my fill of bread and ham and cheese. As I was getting ready to leave, she cut a large hunk of ham off the bone and sliced off a chunk of cheese, wrapping them in paper for me to take with me.

"Pour le petit chat malade," she said, pressing the package into my hands. Then she gave me a stern look. "Get rid of it soon."

When I got home, I took some photos of Georgie and wrote up some text for a flyer. All of this was enough motivation to get me up the next morning, and drag myself into work. I wanted to run the flyer past my colleague Marie-Thérèse and also use the printer and photocopier at work to make copies.

Marie-Thérèse was sympathetic, as usual. She corrected my French on the flyer and gave me some tips to make it more appealing. She and her boyfriend had a couple of dogs and so they weren't interested in adopting a cat, but she promised to mention Georgie and his situation to friends. I printed out the finished copy of the flyer and then made forty photocopies. I put one on the staff bulletin board in the break room and stuffed the rest of them in a folder which I put in my backpack along with a stapler and a tape dispenser I'd taken from my desk. I could hear Marie-Claude's voice coming down the hall as I headed to the door and so I narrowly missed running into her on my way out.

I decided to concentrate posting the flyers in my own neighborhood, as that was where Georgie was from and it would be easiest to turn him over to someone in the area. I stapled my flyer to wooden poles and fences, and taped them on metal rails and the sides of bus kiosks. I asked some shopkeepers in the area to post them in their windows for me and several of them obliged. I even taped one to the wall where I'd climbed up to pet Georgie, along with his mother and siblings, at the very start of this adventure. I knew that the flyer wouldn't stay up very long but I felt I had to post one there on principle.

When I got back home, I tried calling two more animal shelters and got more or less the same answer that I'd gotten from the first place I talked to. It seemed that there was no solution for poor people to surrender their animals in the greater Paris region, other than to dump them on the street. It was discouraging, but I tried to remain hopeful that the right person would see one of the flyers.

Later I talked to Julie on the phone. She was pleased to hear of the developments on my end and my efforts to find Georgie a new home. We settled on a date for me to return to Boston, and when I checked my computer awhile later, there was already a copy of the travel itinerary from the airline in my email. Now the fact that I was leaving Paris seemed solid and real; I now had a hard deadline for dealing with all my loose ends in Paris, including finding a new home for my feline pal.

By now, I didn't see any point in going back into work for any reason, other than to pick up my final paycheck. So, I stopped in one day to collect that check, and to clean out my desk and say good-bye to Marie-Thérèse and a couple of other co-workers who'd been friendly to me during my time there.

I also stopped by the photocopier and made another twenty copies of my flyer. I was hoping to not have to see Marie-Claude while I was there, but this time she proved impossible to avoid. She came into the copy room just as I'd finished stuffing the flyers into my backpack. She was surprisingly cordial to me and seemed to be genuine in thanking me for all the work I'd done on the project. That caught me a little off guard, and caused me to venture telling her about Georgie and my need to find a home for him before I left.

"A cat?" she said, wrinkling her nose in disgust. "No, I definitely wouldn't want one of those dirty animals and I can't think of anyone I know who would."

That was the final nail in the coffin for any stray good thoughts I might have entertained about Marie-Claude. I abruptly ended the conversation there, and walked out of that office with the intention to never darken the door again.

Since I was in town, I decided to go by the anarchist bookstore that I sometimes visited. Marie-France had connections there, and I'd had an article published in their monthly newspaper the year before. I'd also bought plenty of books and other materials from there during my time in Paris. I didn't recognize the person on staff when I walked in, but he was friendly enough and willing to engage in a conversation with me despite my poor French. I explained Georgie's situation to him and made a case for Georgie being an "anarchist cat" as best I could, just for some light humor. He took two of the flyers, promising to put one in the window and to make additional copies for the literature table with the other.

I thanked him and was starting to leave when he stopped me. "Hey, you know what?' he said. "Jean-Michele is in the back, in the radio studio, doing his show. I can ask if he'd interrupt and let you do an announcement about the cat."

"Oh, I don't know," I replied, feeling shy at the thought of being on the radio. "My French is terrible, and I wouldn't know what to say."

"Just hold on; let me ask him." Then he was on the phone, talking rapidly to someone who I assumed was Jean-Michele in the back. I couldn't catch most of what he was saying, but I did hear the phrase "*chat anarchiste*" at least twice.

"Yeah, yeah, it's OK, yes, go on back," he told me when he got off the phone, smiling and waving me toward a door at the back of the shop.

"But, my French..." I started.

"It's OK, you can speak in English. Jean-Michele will translate for you and people will understand; just go on back."

With some trepidation, I went to the door and entered the studio space for on *Radio Libertaire*, the anarchist station operated by the same collective that ran the bookstore. A young man with curly dark hair invited me in, and pointed to a seat next to him at the console. A record was spinning on a turntable, and I could hear the muted sounds of the thrash punk song that playing.

"We go on at the end of this song, OK?" Jean-Michele said to me. "Just pause every once in awhile and let me translate."

"OK," I replied back, feeling somewhat panicked and backed into a corner.

When the song ended, he flipped a switch and spoke into the microphone in front of him on the table. I could pick up some of what he was saying and knew that I was the "Camarade américain" with the "chat anarchiste" that was under discussion.

Then he flipped a switch and a signal button on the microphone on my side of the table lit up. He gestured for me to speak into it.

"Um, hello," I said. "Bonne après-midi. My apologies for addressing you in English. I'm here to tell you about my cat: Georgie, the anarchist cat." I paused and Jean-Michele translated what I said. Then I continued, pausing periodically for Jean-Michele to render what I was saying into French.

"He's very beautiful—black-and-white, with lovely long fur and dark, golden eyes. He has a tear-drop shaped blaze on his chest because he's had cause for tears in his short, hard life. He was born on the street in Noisy-Le-Sec to a homeless single mother…He came into my yard as a starving street cat and I started feeding and caring for him. Then he almost lost his life to rat poison manufactured by the capitalist chemical industry…Thanks to some veterinarian comrades who heroically treated him, his life was saved. He's been living happily with me for the last four months, but I have to return to America and I can't afford to bring him with me… The animal shelters I've contacted are all full or require too big of a payment for me to leave him there. But I can't stand the thought of turning him back out on the street again… If anyone listening to this would like to adopt this brave, beautiful, anarchist cat, I can guarantee that your life will be the better for it." I ended by thanking the listeners and giving out my phone number.

Jean-Michele followed up the final translation by saying something quick about the upcoming music, then flipped switches on the control panel to turn the microphones off and play the next song on the turntable. I shook his hand and thanked him, and gave him one of the flyers. He promised to make additional announcements about the cat when he could.

I felt buoyed by this tremendous support from my anarchist comrades, and it gave me the confidence to enter some of the other shops in the area to ask to leave flyers with them. When I got home later in the day, Georgie was there to greet me as always. I stroked his silky fur and told him, "You might not know it, but people were talking about you on the radio today." He blinked his beautiful golden eyes, rubbed his head against my hand, and started to purr. It felt good just to be around him, but I fought back a sickening feeling in my gut. He loved me and trusted me, but here I was, working to get rid of him. My logical mind kept reminding me that it was really the only way to move forward, but my emotional reaction told me something very different.

My departure date was drawing near. I had sold or given away my surplus books and other belongings. I had whittled down everything I owned to what could fit into two carry-on bags and two oversized duffle bags that would cost me some extra baggage fees. I was cleaning the apartment and scrubbing down the kitchen one last time—I didn't want to leave a mess for Marie-Anne to have to clean up before another tenant could move in. I was saying my good-byes to friends and neighbors, and I was doing some of the things I had been meaning to do since I had arrived twenty months earlier as a new resident. I saw a wildly spectacular performance of Shakespeare's play *Julius Caesar* at the national theater on the Trocadero, and during the intermission I had a coffee by a fifty-foot-tall window that perfectly framed the Eiffel Tower, standing about a block away. I also had an enjoyable evening around the Tuilleries Palace with Marie-Thérèse, her boyfriend, and some other friends during an annual music festival when every musician in France, from the ragged busker in a small town to the national orchestra in the Louvre, turns out and plays for the public, free of charge. There were sentimental tears in my eyes for days on end. It was as though this great enchanted city had dressed to the nines and invited me out, just to say farewell. But how would Paris keep my sweet Georgie?

I continued to brainstorm about where I might leave Georgie. In the Bois de Boulogne, where the prostitutes might feed him? Along the Canal de l'Ourcq, where there were many empty factory buildings where he might take shelter? Maybe somewhere out in the country? Or how about in front of the old cat lady's home? There was a hardcore cat lady in Noisy-le-Sec who walked the streets at 3am with big bags of cat food, making her rounds. I used to listen to her roaring advice about Georgie under the streetlamps—advice I sometimes disagreed with. She was a regular fanatic about how a pet owner should care for their animal. She wouldn't budge on anything even if the humans were poor. Still, I enjoyed talking with her, and she seemed to know every single stray in the town. She wasn't my first choice for a caretaker for Georgie, but at least I could be sure she would feed him.

My shelves were near empty and most of the "to-do" items on my list were crossed off. I was thinking of who I needed to call before the telephone service would be shut off when the phone rang. A man on the line was speaking English with a heavy French accent.

"Is Georgie still available?" he asked.

I was astonished. "Yes, yes he is!" I replied. "How do you know about him?"

It turned out that he and his partner had been listening to *Radio Libertaire* and had heard my announcement. He was reminded again that day when Jean-Michele made another public service announcement on the air, and he decided to call. The next day was a Saturday, and the caller asked me to bring Georgie by his apartment so that he and his partner could meet him. I jotted down the address and agreed to bring the cat by at two in the afternoon.

The journey the next day, first by train and then by Metro, was one that took us from the working-class suburb of Noisy-le-Sec in the militantly left-radical outskirts of Seine-Saint-Denis to the 6th arrondissement, or sixth district, one of the oldest and most desirable neighborhoods of Paris proper. A short walk from the Metro stop will take you past the Sorbonne, through Place Saint-Michel, to the Île de la Cité where once upon an ancient time, the sheep and cattle were forded across the river and the original settlement was built along the Seine. This is one of the most expensive neighborhoods in the world, and my Georgie had an appointment there.

After walking a few blocks, I found the right building; it had an impressive stone façade and iron-work railings guarding the small balconies facing the street. After I located the correct doorbell, my cat and I were buzzed in. I carried him up a beautiful but tight spiral staircase to the third floor. At the top of the landing we were warmly greeted by two men in their thirties who welcomed me into their small but pleasant apartment. It was tastefully decorated with new, comfortable furniture and had an impressive collection of art on the wall. There were sliding glass doors at the back of the living room which opened onto a small balcony overlooking the interior courtyard of the building. It was a clean and safe place for a cat to enjoy basking in the sunlight. Jean-Bernard, who was the one I'd spoken to on the phone, shook my hand and introduced me to his partner Jean-Luc and their cat Luna. She was all black and very calm and friendly, but was a bit wary upon seeing a new animal entering her space.

This is one of the most expensive neighborhoods in the world,
and my Georgie had an appointment there.

Jean-Bernard spoke English fairly well and served as a translator between myself and Jean-Luc. They graciously served coffee and biscuits while the two cats eyed each other. I was impressed by how smoothly they navigated the economic divide between us. Jean-Bernard mentioned that it was customary for the giver of a cat to bring all the veterinary care up to date before the animal was transferred, but under the circumstances they offered to take care of all that. I was grateful, of course, because this was one more thing that I hadn't even thought of and obviously couldn't afford. When I took the half-bag of cat food that I still had left out of my backpack, both men stared at it, surprised. "Oh, we'll find a use for it," said Jean-Bernard without much conviction. It was bottom-shelf crap that cost one euro per three-pound bag, and I realized that they would probably not dream of feeding it to their cats. Instead, it might get tossed to the pigeons or most likely just thrown in the trash.

They immediately took a liking to Georgie and were very interested in his awful adventure with the poison. We sipped coffee in their lovely apartment and made small talk as the cats slowly became more acquainted with each other. I finally asked my hosts, "So, you two are anarchists, then?"

"Well, no. Why do you ask?"

"You said that you heard about Georgie on *Radio Libertaire*, the anarchist station, so I just assumed."

"Oh, no. We just like the music they play." Jean-Bernard said that they had been very moved by my impassioned announcement, and that they had been talking for a while about finding a companion for Luna. She was lonely and depressed when they were both at work or traveling. Hearing my announcement seemed like a sign and made them think that they could possibly help solve two problems at once.

The problem that had been weighing on me had indeed been solved. As hard as it was to say one last "good-bye" to him and rub his beautiful head one last time, I left the apartment with the knowledge that Georgie had a new, good home. A huge burden was lifted from my heart.

A couple of short days later, I was on a trans-Atlantic flight headed to Boston. As the plane lifted up from Charles de Gaulle Airport, I looked down on Paris for my final glimpse of the beautiful City of Lights. I couldn't quite pick out where, but I knew that somewhere in that maze of streets, in one of the toniest neighborhoods of Paris, if not the world, a beautiful black-and-white cat was now poised to live the good life. As for me, I was still poor, drunk, and down on my luck—but I was heading home to my next adventure and happy in the knowledge that I had some good friends who would be standing by my side.

* * * * *

Six months later, I was pretty much settled back into life in Boston. I'd stayed in my friend Damien's spare room for about a month and then moved to a cheap boarding house in the neighborhood. I was barely eking out a living doing construction jobs and the occasional writing gig. It was hard to make ends meet and going hungry was once again a real concern. The local Food Not Bombs collective served a meal at the anarchist community space twice a month. I showed up to volunteer to help with the cooking and serving and cleaning up afterwards but, frankly, I was also there to eat. I gleaned any free food I could from the collective's give-aways, gladly accepted any handouts or free meals from friends, and on more than one occasion resorted to dumpster-diving behind restaurants and grocery stores. Admittedly, the situation was worsened by the fact that I often chose booze over food when I had money to spend. I'd gone through a stint in a rehab program and was sober for more than a week, but then fell off the wagon once again.

Julie had been helpful, as usual, and would sometimes "loan" me small sums of money with the full knowledge that she'd probably never get repaid. I still considered her one of my closest friends, but things had definitely changed between us. She'd instituted a "zero tolerance policy" and refused to speak on the phone or be near me in person if I were drunk or hungover, which constituted a large portion of my waking hours. She and her boyfriend were also planning on getting married, so our lives were definitely moving in very different directions now.

Then one evening, I was packaging up some leftovers from the Food Not Bombs meal when Damien walked into the community center and greeted me. "Hey," he said, "I got a letter for you from France that I thought you might want to see." He handed me a rumpled envelope with a colorful canceled stamp on it. When I first landed back in Boston, I had sent postcards to people back in Paris, giving Damien's address as a way to contact me. I got a nice postcard back from Marie-Anne, but mostly didn't hear from anyone. I wasn't sure who was writing to me now, but was pleasantly surprised when I ripped open the envelope.

A color photograph of two cats cuddled up together fell from between a folded sheet of paper. One was a plump black cat and the other was a beautiful long-haired black-and-white cat with a tear-drop-shaped blaze on his chest. Georgie! He'd put on some weight since I'd said good-bye to him and his fur seemed to glisten. Tears rose to my eyes as I beheld my anarchist cat once again. Then I took a look at the letter enclosed, which read:

Hello, our American Friend! We were listening to *Radio Libertaire* a few days since and thought of you. I found your post card and thought you might enjoy this photo to send to you. Jo-Jo as we call him now is doing very well, healthy and happy! He and Luna are in love! As you can see in the photo. Thank you for bringing him into our lives, we are loving him so much. Thanks again and take care!

Your friends in Paris,
Jean-Bernard and Jean-Luc

I turned away and wiped the tears from my face with the back of my hand. I realized that even though I was still down on my luck and struggling, I'd at least done one thing right in my life, or maybe even two. I'd helped save Georgie's life when he'd been poisoned and I had managed to save him again from the mean streets of Noisy-Le-Sec. I was overcome with emotion to think of him now, so happy and healthy, with an affectionate cat friend and living with people who loved him and took such good care of him. Georgie was living the good life in Paris, something that had eluded me. But seeing him again gave me a glimmer of hope that maybe, just maybe, life could get better for me as well.

Enjoyed this story? Read more from Frayed Edge Press...

Literature

Ambushing the Void short stories by James McAdams
¿Cómo Hacer Preguntas? or How To Make Questions: 69 Instructional Poems (in English) by Daniel Hales
Bellapalma by Jens Bjørneboe; translated by Esther Greenleaf Mürer
Ere the Cock Crows by Jens Bjørneboe; translated and with a reconstruction of the play by Esther Greenleaf Mürer
Rape Jokes by Louise MacGregor
Stealing: A Novel in Dreams by Shelly Brivic
The Splooge Factory poety by Christina Springer

History and Politics

"Do Not Misunderstand Me": The Collected Radical Addresses to the Unity Congregation (1888-1891) by Hugh Owen Pentecost
Jeremiah Hacker: Journalist, Anarchist, Abolitionist by Rebecca Pritchard
A Nurse's Story: Medical Missionary in Korea and Siberia, 1915-1920 by Delia Battles Lewis

Street Smart Series -- Short Fiction for People on the Go

Full Fare by Jean-Bernard Pouy
Down and Out in Paris, with Cat by R.A. Bolo
The Accidental Anarchist by A.R. Melnik
Stealing MacGuffin by Matthew Kastel
Pele's Domain by Albert Tucher

Visit us at: https://www.frayededgepress.com/